The Hill
and the Rock

The rights of David McKee to be identified as the author and illustrator of this work have
been asserted by him in accordance with the Copyright, Designs and Patents Act, 1988.
First published in Great Britain in 1984 by Andersen Press Ltd., 20 Vauxhall Bridge Road,
London SW1V 2SA.
This paperback edition first published in 1997 by Andersen Press Ltd.
Published in Australia by Random House Australia Pty., 20 Alfred Street, Milsons Point,
Sydney, NSW 2061. All rights reserved. Colour separated in Switzerland by Photolitho AG,
Offsetreproduktionen, Gossau, Zürich. Printed and bound in Italy by Grafiche AZ, Verona.

10   9   8   7   6   5   4   3   2   1

British Library Cataloguing in Publication Data available.

ISBN 0 86264 784 3

This book has been printed on acid-free paper

The Hill
and the Rock

David McKee

Andersen Press London

Mr and Mrs Quest lived in a little house on the very top of a hill, the only hill in that part of the country.

Because it was the only hill there were lots of visitors. The views were wonderful.

Getting to the top of the hill was a bit hard for the visitors, but going home was easy. Everyone said it was a perfect place to live.

"It would be perfect," said Mrs Quest to her husband, "if it wasn't for the rock."

The rock stood at the back of the house and blocked half of
the view from the kitchen window.

"It is perfect," said Mr Quest. "Half of our view is better
than the whole of anyone else's view."

"Besides," said Mr Quest, "I can climb on top of the rock and see even further."

But Mrs Quest kept on about the rock. "You can go to work, but I have to stay and look at that rock," or "I spend a lot of time in that kitchen," and often just "It's a pity about the rock."

Eventually one night Mr Quest said, "I'll see about it tomorrow," and Mrs Quest was happy.

The next day Mr Quest dug away the ground outside the rock. Then he pushed it from the other side. The rock rolled all the way to the bottom of the hill.

"Hurrah!" cheered Mr Quest.

Mrs Quest was delighted now she had a full view from the kitchen window. But that night she said, "What's that funny hissing sound?" Her husband, who was tired out from his hard work, was already fast asleep.

The following night it was Mr Quest who said, "What's that funny hissing sound?"

"I don't know," said Mrs Quest, "but I heard it last night as well."

The day after that, Mr Quest thought it seemed easier going home from work. When he arrived home, he found his wife crying.

"The hill is going down," she sobbed. "The hissing is the air in the hill escaping from the hole where the rock was."

Sure enough, day after day, night after night, the hill went down, until one day it was gone altogether.

"Now we're just the same as everyone else," said Mr Quest.

Visitors still came out of curiosity, but they didn't stay long. There was nothing to see. "Nice day," they would say, and go on their way.

Poor Mrs Quest! Without the hill there wasn't any view, except from the kitchen window where she could still see the rock in the distance. And the hissing still did not stop.

Day and night, night and day, the house still kept going down
until it was at the bottom of a valley.

Visitors came, for after all, it was the only valley in that part of the country and it was easy to get there. They didn't stay long. The side of a valley isn't much of a view, and it was hard work to go home.

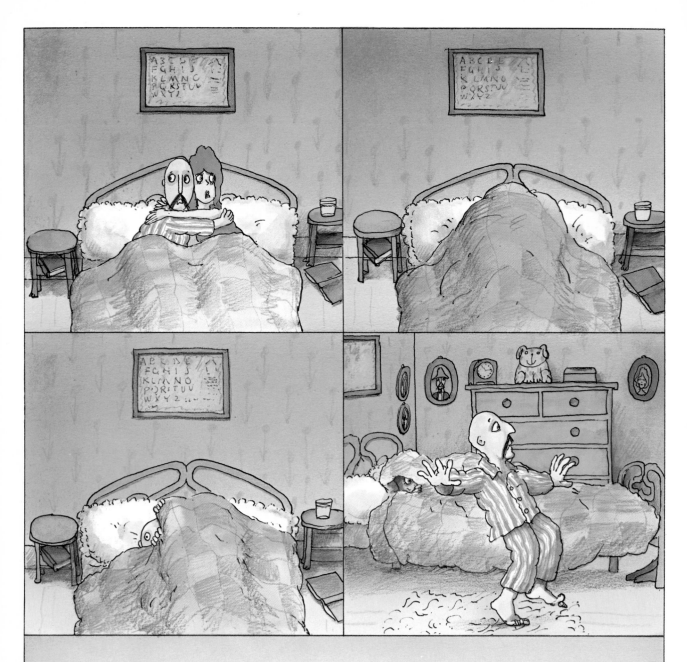

One night a new noise frightened Mr and Mrs Quest. A terrible rumbling and a crash. Mr Quest peeped out from under the bedclothes and then went to see what was happening.

In the dark, he could not see a thing. He bolted the door, hurried back to bed and hid under the covers again.

In the morning, Mr Quest looked carefully outside. "It's the rock!" he shouted to Mrs Quest. "It's rolled down the valley and back into the hole!"

"Oh no! It's worse than before!" said Mrs Quest. "Now it covers the whole of the kitchen window."

"Never mind," said Mr Quest, "I have an idea."

For the rest of the day, he worked at the back of the rock.

When he had finished, he had painted a picture on the rock. "Now at least the kitchen has a view," he said.

Mrs Quest was pleased. "And the hissing has stopped," she said.

Now that the air couldn't escape, the house started to rise again. Day and night, the valley gradually disappeared. The house continued to rise until finally the hill was back in its old place.

Once again, the visitors began to trek up the only hill in that part of the country.

"You are lucky," they said to Mrs Quest. "It's a perfect place to live with such wonderful views."

"Perfect," agreed Mrs Quest, "and my favourite view is the one from the kitchen window. Come and see."